ISBN-13: 978-1523851669
ISBN-10: 152385166X

MABEL

and the

SOCK
PIRATES

By
Elwyn
Tate

Up on a **hill**
lived a farmer
called **Bill**...

...and a black and
white cat
called
Mabel.

They **had cows...**

...they had **sheep...**

and **some**
hay in
a heap...

...which **they**
fed to
a **horse** in
a **stable.**

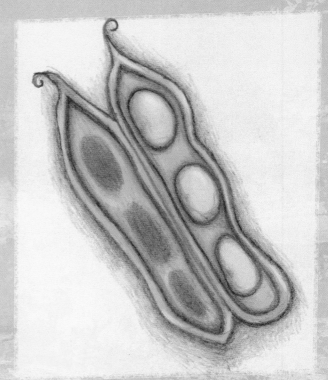

They **had apples...** and **beans,**

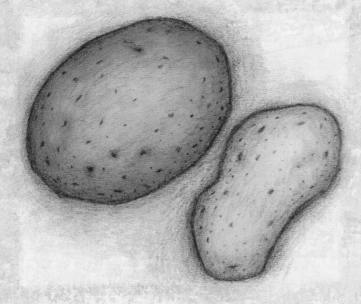

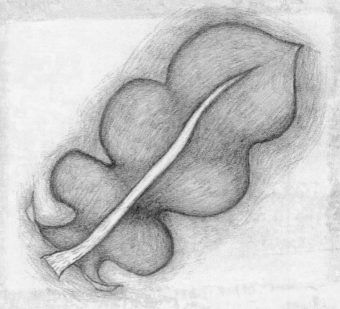

potatoes... and greens,

were their magical trees...

which grew **socks!**

There were red socks and green socks.

Long socks and lean socks.

There were socks
made of silver
and gold.

They were
stripey...

and spotty.

Chequered...

and
dotty.

While **some** were just **smelly** and **old**.

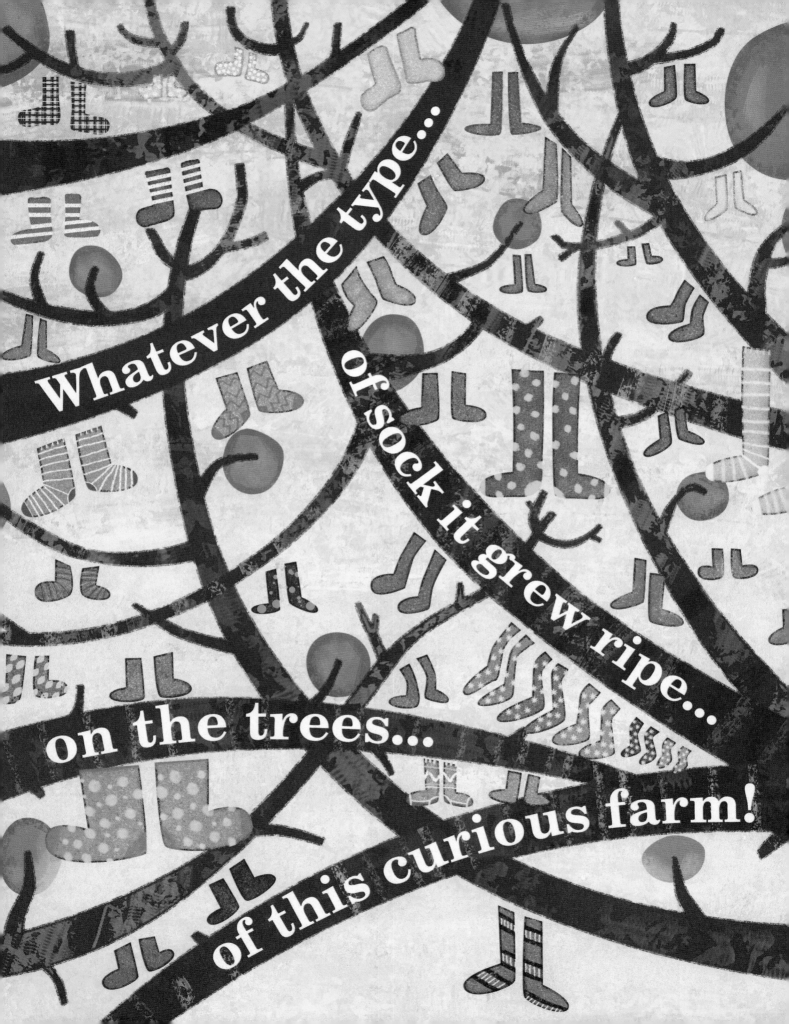

Whatever the type...
of sock it grew ripe...
on the trees...
of this curious farm!

And Bill liked to stroll through his orchard at night

with Mabel curled up on his arm.

BUT!

It was **late** one July when **pirates** sailed by, and they **spied** on the magical **trees.**

"Yo Ho!"
said the chief
(that dastardly thief)
"Let's take
all the
socks that
we please."

So up the crooks crept while Farmer Bill slept...

...and they **pilfered** and **plundered** with **glee.**

But watching this **theft**, with marvelous **deft**, was **Mabel**... high up **in a tree.**

"Oh what a scene...

...those pirates are mean,"

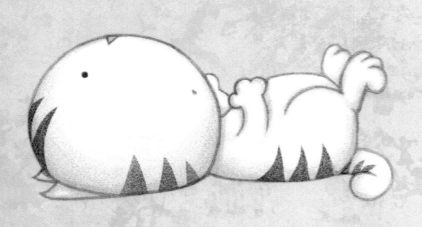 

she said in a
terrible huff.

"They're stealing
and **looting,**

they're laughing
and **hooting,**

and I...

have had...

**quite
enough!"**

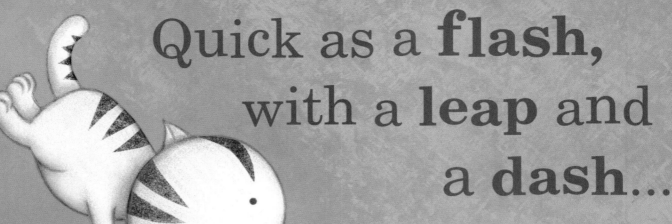

Quick as a **flash,**
with a **leap** and
a **dash**...

But she
tripped...

on a jumble...
of socks...

...she **ran** yelling,

"Stop pirates
...**HALT!**"

...and turned
a complete
somersault.

...with a
tumble...

Mabel the **cat** was covered in **socks,**

from her **head,**
to her **paws,**
to her **tail.**

Still she ran **and she** flew at **the** piratical crew, **and she gave an enormous BIG...**

"Yo **HO** pirate boys. What's **making** that **noise**?" said the **chief** as he scratched on his **beard.**

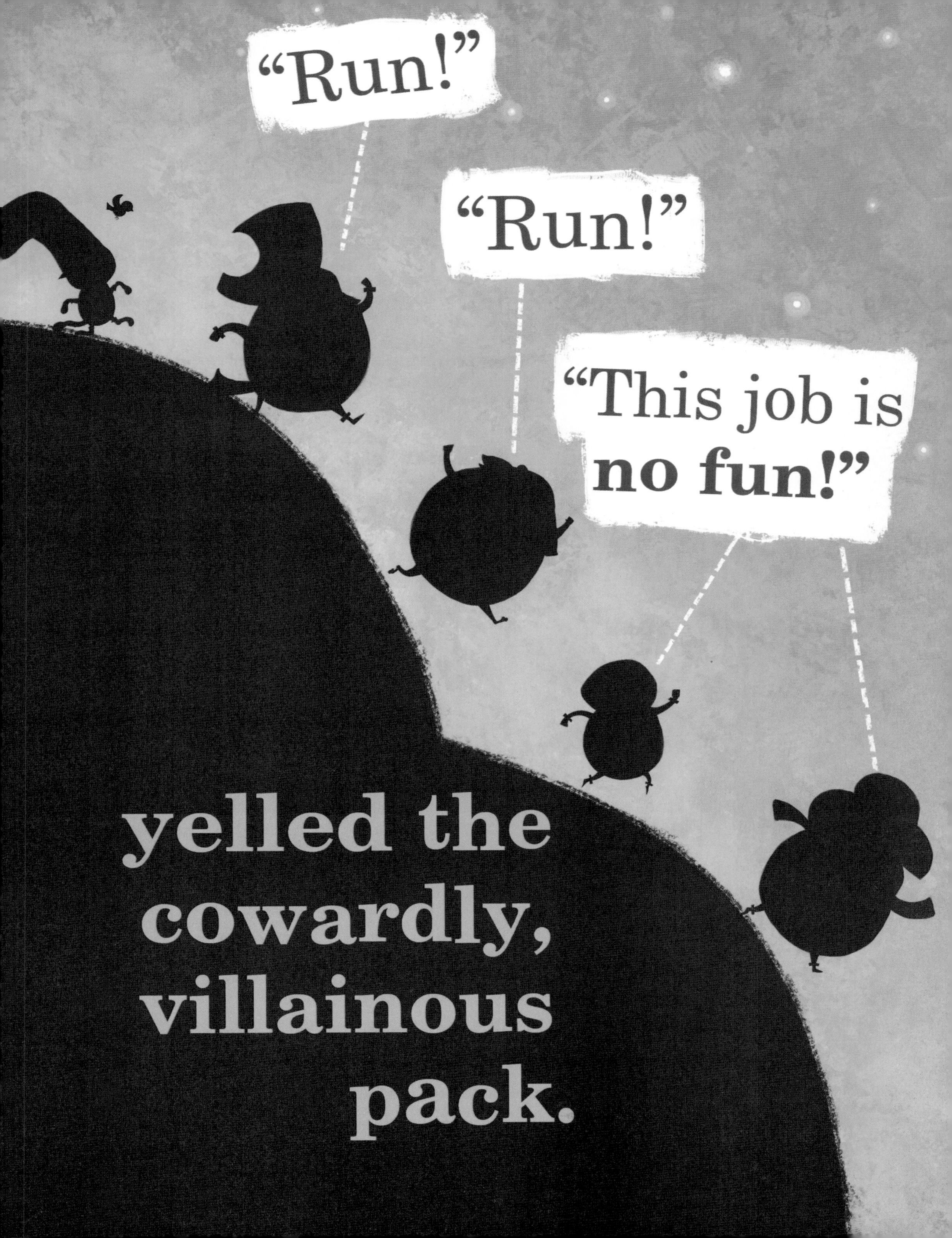

yelled the cowardly, villainous pack.

So they
scampered away
to their boat
in the
bay...

and the
SOCK PIRATES
... never... **came... back.**

Mabel collected...

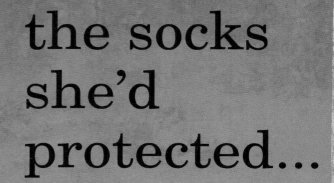

the socks she'd protected...

...and fell fast asleep with a smile.

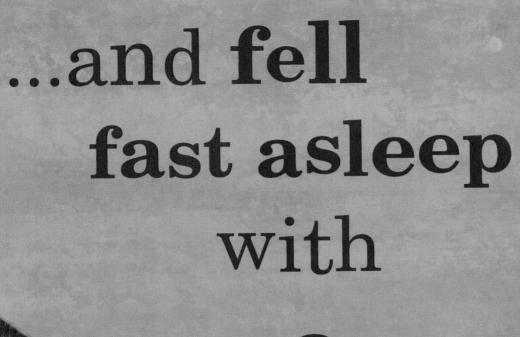

The End

MABEL

Printed in Great Britain
by Amazon

82506728R10033